The Day of the
DODGY DOUBLES

Written by Chris Callaghan and Zoë Clarke

Illustrated by Amit Tayal

Collins

Shinoy and the Chaos Crew

When Shinoy downloads the Chaos Crew app on his phone, a glitch in the system gives him the power to summon his TV heroes into his world.

With the team on board, Shinoy can figure out what dastardly plans the red-eyed S.N.A.I.R., a Super Nasty Artificial Intelligent Robot, has come up with, and save the day.

1 Seeing double

There were four voice messages on Shinoy's phone. They were all from Toby.

"Shinoy, are you there? It's me."

"Hello? Hello? Shinoy?"

"I'm in the park and I've just seen Lazlo and Salama. They're having a picnic with S.N.A.I.R.!"

"Did you press the app button? What's going on?"

Shinoy ran to the park where he found Toby hiding behind a bush.

"I thought you'd been zapped away somewhere!" Toby said.

"I was reading the latest Chaos Crew comic and I put my phone on silent. Why are you hiding?"

Toby pointed. "I'm keeping an eye on them!"

"Lazlo and Salama are having a picnic with S.N.A.I.R.," Shinoy said slowly.

"That's what I said in my message!" Toby spluttered. "What's going on?"

Shinoy shrugged. "No idea, but I bet the others would like to know." He was just about to press the app to call his TV heroes, when he saw Merit and Bug. They were taking selfies!

"There's Harry!" Toby pointed.

Shinoy frowned. "Wait a minute ... that's a poodle."

Toby stifled a laugh. "Don't let Harry hear you call him a poodle!"

"No. That's *actually* a poodle. It's not Harry," Shinoy said.

Toby had a good look. "And *he* looks a bit short to be Merit."

They were interrupted by
a boy. "I can't believe they're
filming the spin-off series of
Chaos Crew in Flat Hill!"

"There is no Chaos Crew
spin-off series," Toby said.

"There is now! Chaos Crew: Flat Hill!
I'm going to get their autographs!"

As they watched the boy run off, Shinoy
pressed the app on his phone. "Time for
the real thing. Call to Action, Chaos Crew!"

2 Chaos Crew: the spin-off

Ember appeared in a flash of light.
"Am I missing something?" she asked,
looking over at the other
Chaos Crew members.

"It's a spin-off Chaos Crew
series," Shinoy told her.

"No one told me," she said.
"Wait a minute
… Merit looks
a bit short. And is
that supposed to be Harry?"
Ember started
laughing. "It's a
… *poodle!*"

"Oh look, it's you," Shinoy said, as another Ember appeared. A photographer had arrived from the *Flat Hill Gazette*. The fake Chaos Crew grouped together and posed.

"We don't do that," Ember said.

Fake Merit lifted fake Salama in the air. Fake Lazlo lifted fake Ember. Fake Bug lifted fake Harry-the-poodle.

Ember sighed, "And we don't do that."

Fake S.N.A.I.R. pranced about trying to look menacing. Shinoy looked at Toby and cracked up. "He does do that."

Harry-the-poodle had got hold of part of fake S.N.A.I.R.'s outfit and was giving it a good tug.

"We should definitely go and say hello," Toby said.

Fake Ember looked Ember up and down. "Nice outfit. Old style."

Ember blinked.

"What happened to the original TV Chaos Crew?" Shinoy asked.

"The production company wanted to update the brand and give it a fresh new look. We're the dynamic young faces of Chaos Crew – the Chaos Club! Gotta run. Filming starts in five!"

"Let's go and watch the *Chaos Club* in action," Shinoy suggested.

Fake Ember was attached to wires. She flapped about in the air, unconvincingly. Fake Merit pretended to fight S.N.A.I.R. They danced around each other, while S.N.A.I.R. fired multi-coloured lights from his gloves, and Merit shouted, "Come and get me!" and "I'm sooo scared." Fake Salama ran around shrieking and fake Bug just wandered off. Fake Harry barked a lot.

Toby stared. "This is so bad."

"Maybe we should check out the production van," Shinoy said. The large black van was parked next to the film crew.

They sidled past the film crew and round the side of the van. They tried the door but it was locked.

"How are we going to get in?" Toby asked.

Ember unpacked her wings. *"Old style."*

Shinoy and Toby watched as Ember spread her wings and rose swiftly into the air. She landed silently on top of the van, opened the roof hatch and climbed in.

There was a CLICK and the door slid open. "Come and look at this," Ember whispered.

The van was filled with monitors.

"Now why would a film company have these?" Ember wondered. "They're Spy Scanners. They're used to scan for People of Interest." She pressed a few buttons.

"It's me!" Shinoy said, as his image flashed up on the screen.

"And me!" Toby said. "Why's Mr Amitri there? He's really not that interesting."

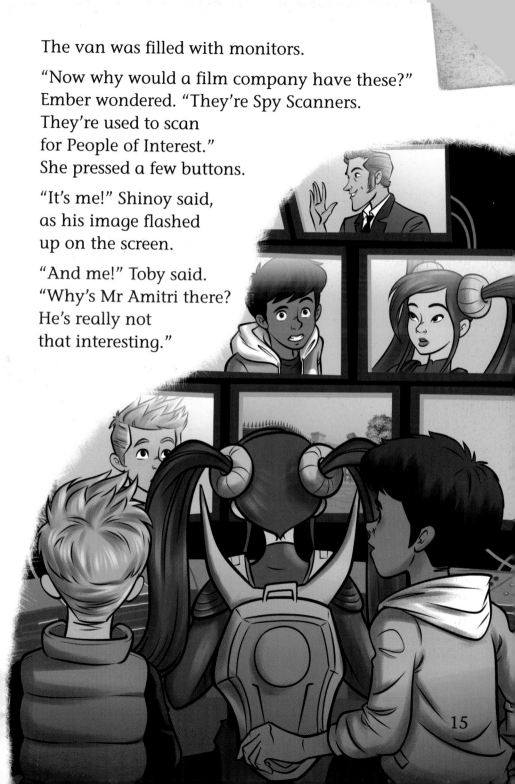

"The filming must be a cover for someone keeping an eye on you," Ember said. "But why make up a Chaos Crew spin-off?"

"I bet the answer's behind that door," Toby said, pointing to the back of the van.

They opened the door slowly. The room beyond was pitch black. Then two red lights shone out.

"Ooh, it's baby S.N.A.I.R.," Shinoy said.

Suddenly, lots of red lights appeared. "Lots of baby S.N.A.I.R.s. Are they props?"

Toby picked up the baby S.N.A.I.R. nearest to him. "I want one!"

"Put it down, very gently," Ember said quietly. "That's an Exploding Clone."

"Putting down the exploding baby S.N.A.I.R. Clone very gently," Toby whispered. "And exiting the van – "

3 Attack of the Exploding Clones

They closed the van door and walked away.
"So the TV van is spy central,"
Shinoy said. "And it's also carrying
lots of Exploding S.N.A.I.R. Clones."

Ember nodded.
"There'll be
a remote control
for the Clones
and we need to
find it."

"Those actors are
so bad, they must
be S.N.A.I.R. spies.
Maybe they're
going to release
the Clones
during filming?"
Toby guessed.

"Agreed," Ember said. "No one would
realise it's a Flat Hill takeover until
it was too late."

Shinoy suddenly went pale. "Wait a minute. Who's the only 'actor' who's doing what they usually do?"

At that moment, S.N.A.I.R. turned to look at them and grinned.

4 Hunt for S.N.A.I.R.

"We can't let him release the Exploding Clones!" Ember said.

Shinoy started running. "I'm getting that remote from him!"

Just then, the director shouted, "Cut!" and the filming stopped. A group of Chaos Crew fans, who'd been waiting on the other side of the park, rushed towards the fakes. They were each dressed as their favourite Chaos Crew character. Shinoy stopped running. Which one was the real S.N.A.I.R.?

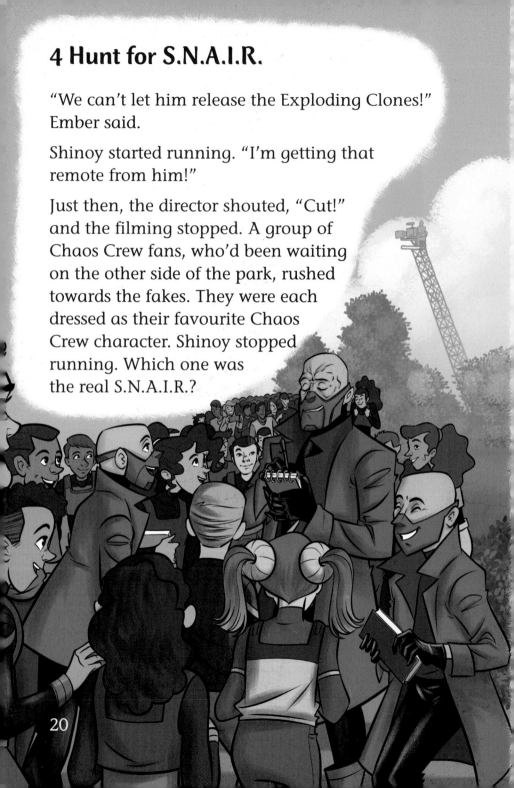

Ember shot up into the sky to get a better view. "The one on the left!"

Toby ran to the left and grabbed a S.N.A.I.R.

"Not that left!" Ember shouted.

Shinoy grabbed another S.N.A.I.R.

Ember flew down. "The other one!"

Toby let his S.N.A.I.R. go. "There are too many S.N.A.I.R.s!"

21

"He's *there*!" Shinoy shouted.

They cornered him by the park gates.

"You fools!" S.N.A.I.R. laughed, pressing the remote control. "I've won at last! *Mwah ha ha ha*!"

Toby looked at Shinoy. "Did he really just do the evil laugh?"

Shinoy shook his head. "So unoriginal."

"How DARE you mock me!" howled S.N.A.I.R., stamping his foot.

"Did you just stamp your foot?" Toby asked. "You aren't very good at this."

Ember swooped down. "Exploding Clones coming this way!"

Toby and Shinoy turned to look as Exploding Clones poured out of the van. They could hear cries of "Ooh, baby S.N.A.I.R.!" coming from the Chaos Crew fans. When they turned back, S.N.A.I.R. had disappeared.

Shinoy looked around desperately. "Where's he gone?"

Ember perched on top of the park gates. "We'll find him later. We need to catch these Clones first."

The Clones turned and headed for Shinoy and Toby.

Toby pointed. "I think they're out to catch us."

"Of course! Your faces were on the Spy Scanner, so once the Clones are activated, they're programmed to find you."

"And what happens when they find us?" Toby asked, in a nervous voice.

"Well," Ember started, "they are *Exploding* Clones. So – "

"Can you use fire on them?" Shinoy asked.

"That will set off too many explosions," Ember said. "I have another idea."

Ember started to glow. She touched the park railings with her hands and the metal heated up and expanded. The spikes bent over and trapped the Clones before they got to them.

"That's amazing!" Toby whooped.

Shinoy squinted. "Where's that one going?"

A single Clone was zooming off in another direction.

"There was only one other person identified on the Spy Scanner," Ember said.

Shinoy gulped, "Mr Amitri!" He and Toby ran off after the last Clone.

They didn't have far to go before they found Mr Amitri. He was cowering behind a tree as the Clone fired lasers at him. Then the Clone started to crackle and fizz.

The explosion seemed to happen in slow motion.

The heat from the blast sent a wave of hot air over everyone.

Shinoy and Toby grabbed a bin and popped it over the Clone.

Ember grabbed Mr Amitri by his jacket and pulled him backwards.

"What is the *meaning* of this?" Mr Amitri spluttered.

"They're filming the Chaos Crew TV show in the park and this prop malfunctioned," Shinoy said. He saw S.N.A.I.R. lurking nearby. "And *he's* in charge!"

Mr Amitri straightened his tie and squared up to S.N.A.I.R. "This is an *absolute disgrace*! Do you hear me?"

"Yes," S.N.A.I.R. said, in a small voice.

Mr Amitri marched S.N.A.I.R. off, muttering about how many laws he'd probably broken.

Shinoy, Ember and Toby creased up with laughter. "S.N.A.I.R. versus Mr Amitri!" Shinoy giggled. "Now *that's* a spin-off I'd like to see."

Ideas for reading

Written by Clare Dowdall, PhD
Lecturer and Primary Literacy Consultant

Reading objectives

- discuss and clarify the meanings of words, linking new meanings to known vocabulary
- make inferences on the basis of what is being said and done
- answer and ask questions
- explain and discuss their understanding of books, poems and other material, both those that they listen to and those that they read for themselves.

Spoken language objectives

- ask relevant questions to extend their understanding and knowledge
- give well-structured descriptions and explanations
- participate in discussions, presentations, performances and debates

Curriculum links: English – composing – write for different purposes (playscript)

Word count: 1,617

Interest words: menacing, dynamic, fake, unoriginal, cowering, lurking

Resources: paper and pencils, large paper and colouring pens

Build a context for reading

- Read the title *The Day of the Dodgy Doubles*. Ask children to suggest what they think a double is – and what it might mean for the story.
- Look at the front cover. Challenge children to say three things that they can see and to raise three questions about what they can see, e.g. Shinoy looking confused ... Why is Shinoy confused?
- Read the back cover blurb. Use the information to deduce what a spin-off is.